Little Netta's
GIFT

This book is a gift of love...

For: _____

From: _____

by Mike Brown   illustrated by Selim Nurudeen

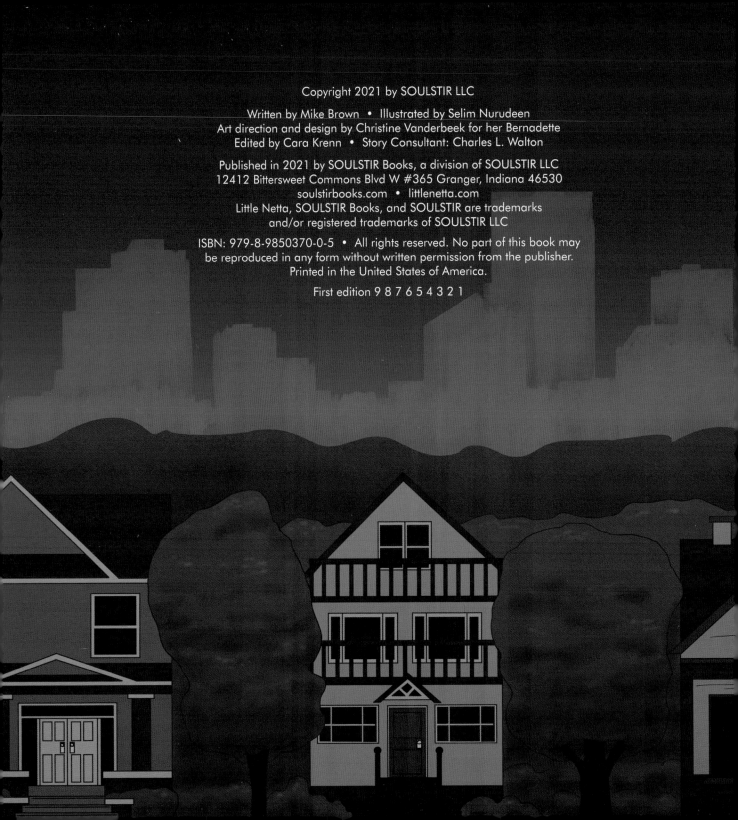

Copyright 2021 by SOULSTIR LLC

Written by Mike Brown • Illustrated by Selim Nurudeen
Art direction and design by Christine Vanderbeek for her Bernadette
Edited by Cara Krenn • Story Consultant: Charles L. Walton

Published in 2021 by SOULSTIR Books, a division of SOULSTIR LLC
12412 Bittersweet Commons Blvd W #365 Granger, Indiana 46530
soulstirbooks.com • littlenetta.com
Little Netta, SOULSTIR Books, and SOULSTIR are trademarks
and/or registered trademarks of SOULSTIR LLC

ISBN: 979-8-9850370-0-5 • All rights reserved. No part of this book may
be reproduced in any form without written permission from the publisher.
Printed in the United States of America.

First edition 9 8 7 6 5 4 3 2 1

"Little Netta,
Little Netta,
please go to sleep."

"But I'm too excited mom.
It's my favorite week!

Tomorrow is Christmas!
Then my sixth birthday.

I can't wait for my friends
to come over and play!"

"I've been a good girl.
I've said all my prayers.

I'll soon open my gifts
from the tree downstairs."

Now Netta's sound asleep,
her heart filled with hope.

She dreams of new toys,
maybe a jump rope!

Christmas Day arrives...
and oh, what joy!

"I got everything
I wanted...

every single toy!"

"A game, a doll,
and a new hat.

More in two days!
How awesome is that?"

Now at Little Netta's party—

friends sing "Happy Birthday!"
She blows out the candles
and hands out the cake.

Netta opens her gifts,
then passes them around,

Together they play...

'til she sees
them frown.

Something is wrong.

Netta asks, "Why so blue?"

They tell her and she thinks,

"I know what
to do."

Then one by one,
the children head home,
with Netta's toys
in their hands—

what's going on?

"Thank you,
Little Netta!"

Her friends all cheer.

"You've really made
this the BEST
time of year!"

Little Netta waves goodbye,
a proud look on her face.

But wait—
uh oh...

What's her
mom
gonna say?

"Little Netta," says her mom,
"Why'd you give your toys away?
Those gifts were for Christmas
and your birthday."

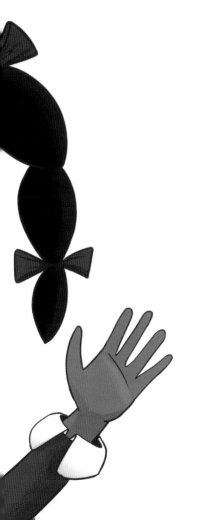

"They had no gifts this year,
and that's not fair!

But I had two sets of toys,
and I wanted to share!"

Her mom hugs Netta,
wipes a tear, and smiles,

So proud of her kind
and giving child.

You can be like Little Netta
no matter your age.

What can you do
to show love today?

LITTLE NETTA'S GIFT is based on a true story
about a caring and beautiful little girl named
Jeannetta Lacole Robinson
and her remarkable act of kindness.

Her birthday is two days after Christmas, and at her sixth birthday party she showed tremendous compassion for others. She gave her gifts to children attending her party after learning they did not receive Christmas gifts.

Jeannetta was from Milwaukee, Wisconsin and part of a strong family of trailblazers whose lives have been centered on serving others. Ms. Cheryl Robinson, an education advocate and court stenographer, was her mom. Commissioner Jeannetta Simpson-Robinson, her namesake and grandmother, was a community leader and Co-Founder and Chief Executive Officer of Career Youth Development, Inc (CYD), a social service organization that worked with youth, adults and families to address multi-faceted problems. The Jeannetta Simpson-Robinson Memorial Highway, named in her honor, is the first memorial highway in Wisconsin that recognizes a woman of color. Ms. Claretta "Mother Freedom" Simpson was her great-grandmother, Co-Founder of CYD, and a civil rights leader who marched in cities across the United States, including Birmingham, AL, Detroit, MI and Washington, DC. Elder Charles L. Walton, a community leader and former CEO of CYD, producer, composer, and musician, is her uncle. Mike Brown, the author of this book and first Black student to portray the University of Notre Dame's Leprechaun mascot, is her cousin.

This book is a tribute to Jeannetta and her gift of love.

May her story serve as inspiration for you to share your gifts with others.